Rained Out

MW00881828

needle

seal

saucepan

crescent
moon

slice of bread

pie

hammer

mushroom

pencil

snail

seashell

pine tree

mouse

Can you find these hidden pictures?

carrot

tulip

sailboat

flag

artist's
brush

nail

fish

bat

Highlights®

duck

toothbrush

lollipop

spool of thread

artist's brush

Can you find these hidden pictures?

comb

banana

teacup

fork

whistle

slice of lemon

carrot

Clowns on Wheels

egg

duck

ring

teacup

book

heart

banana

crescent moon

toothbrush

fish

cat

boot

magnifying glass

pencil

spatula

sailboat

hammer

Can you find these hidden pictures?

Illustrated by Timothy Davis

Highlights®

Brushing Bunny

telephone receiver

closed umbrella

fork

Can you find these hidden pictures?

iron

bell

nail

hammer

spoon

mug

pennant

key

mitten

bird

Rainy Day Friends

Can you find these hidden pictures?

snail · tack · seal · caterpillar · clarinet · heart · ice skate · candle · duck · lizard · 2 birds · fish · whale · mushroom · squirrel · lamp · sailboat · giraffe · pitcher

Illustrated by Linda Weller

Highlights®

fork

drinking straw

book

toothbrush

pennant

golf club

Can you find these hidden pictures?

candle

nail

clothespin

pencil

fishhook

crown

light bulb

frying pan

needle

BIG TALENT SHOW TONIGHT

Highlights®

World Environment Day is June 5.

heart

boot

toothbrush

spoon

musical note

megaphone

banana

bowling pin

snake

comb

Can you find these hidden pictures?

needle

pencil

pliers

bird

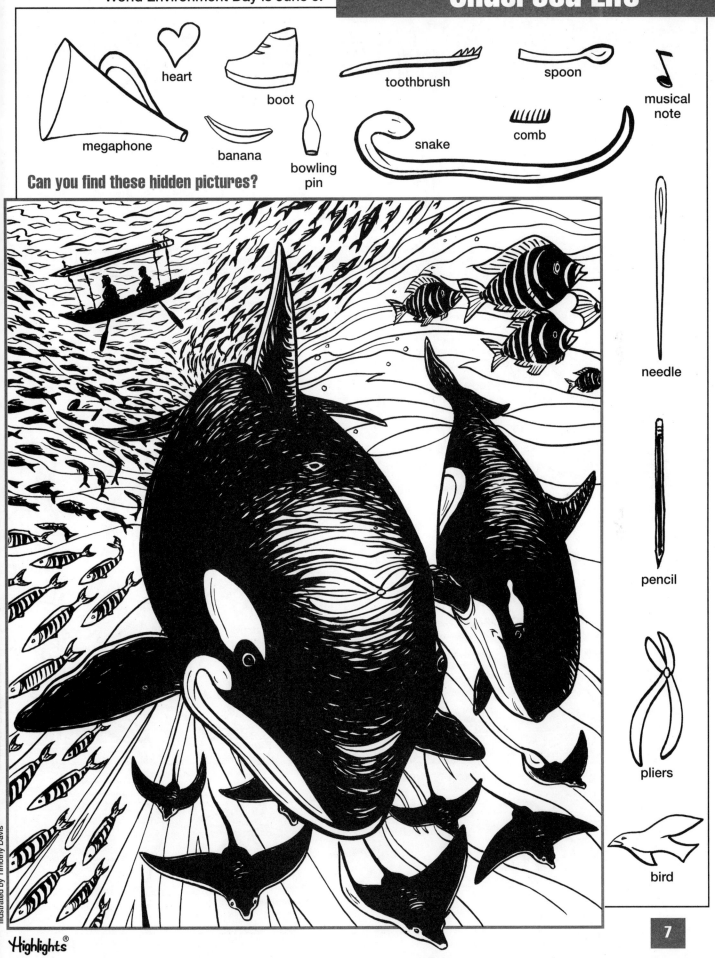

Illustrated by Timothy Davis

Highlights®

sock

heart

fork

ice-cream
cone

paper clip

spoon

ring

crescent
moon

Can you find these hidden pictures?

toothbrush

artist's brush

penguin

scissors

duck

feather

June is National Rose Month.

Ready for Roses

mushroom

ladle

goose

banana

measuring cup

chisel

mug

slice of pie

slice of orange

wishbone

recorder

carrot

flashlight

sock

Can you find these hidden pictures?

BONEMEAL

ROSE FOOD

Illustrated by Elizabeth Allyn

Highlights®

April 2 is International Children's Book Day.

slice of pizza

fishhook

arrow

hammer

dustpan

pennant

Can you find these hidden pictures?

duck

hairbrush

sailboat

mouse

fork

hanger

handbell

ladle

Highlights®

Cardboard Racers

needle

mushroom

apple core

banana

spoon

mug

fish

Can you find these hidden pictures?

toothbrush

screw

pencil

hairbrush

pea pod

Three Men in a Tub

apple

crayon

crescent moon

fishhook

needle

bird

birdhouse

sailboat

artist's brush

mug

Can you find these hidden pictures?

ghost

nail

cake

saucepan

seashell

slice of pie

knitted cap

mushroom

whale

wishbone

Highlights®

July is National Blueberries Month.

Blueberry Lovers

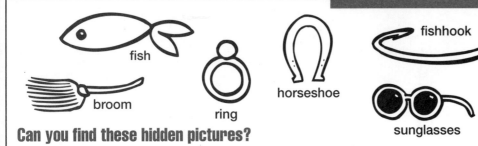

fish

broom

ring

horseshoe

fishhook

sunglasses

bell

sock

Can you find these hidden pictures?

bird

mitten

needle

toothbrush

snail

closed umbrella

telephone receiver

mitten

nail

ring

Can you find these hidden pictures?

fishhook

boot

hanger

3 birds

ant

iron

shovel

pennant

eyeglasses

hairbrush

2 ice-cream cones

turtle

saw

crab

key

frog

Illustrated by Valeri Gorbachev

mushroom

sailboat

turtle

ring

crescent moon

ice-cream cone

Can you find these hidden pictures?

alligator

barbell

dog bone

mitten

shovel

knitted cap

hairbrush

caterpillar

The astronomer who invented the centigrade thermometer was born 300 years ago in 1701.

Anders Celsius of Sweden

teacup

slipper

turtle

toothbrush

spatula

candle

power drill

pyramid

tack

Can you find these hidden pictures?

needle

ice-cream cone

pencil

hockey stick

sailboat

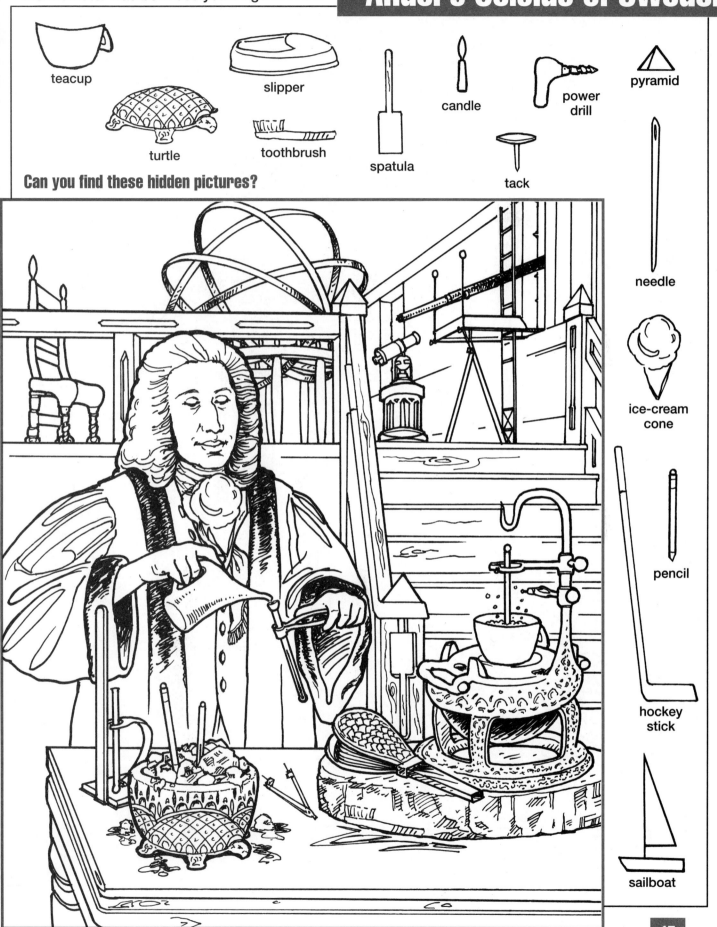

Highlights®

pencil

ballpoint pen

golf club

spoon

flower

Can you find these hidden pictures?

pushpin

needle

banana

eyeglasses

bell

safety pin

wishbone

artist's brush

Illustrated by Charles Jordan

Sandy Creations

sailboat

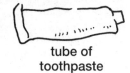
toothbrush

slice of bread

tube of toothpaste

teacup

feather

Can you find these hidden pictures?

party hat

ice-cream pop

heart

domino

eraser

bowl

The Final Leg

snake

needle

penguin

seashell

Can you find these hidden pictures?

party hat

cowboy hat

knitting needle

nail

bell

canoe

dolphin

radish

golf club

hockey stick

artist's brush

pennant

vase

fishhook

funnel

light bulb

drinking glass

carrot

spoon

screw

hat

Illustrated by Janet Robertson

Highlights®

Fall begins on September 22, 2001.

vase

sailboat

mouse

pennant

hairbrush

paper clip

Can you find these hidden pictures?

seal

duck

bow

boot

fork

bird

turtle

stork

In 1851—150 years ago—the schooner won the first of what is now known as the America's Cup.

handbell

needle

pail

banana

loaf of bread

shuttlecock

bird's head

tack

egg

hanger

Can you find these hidden pictures?

party hat

crescent moon

bottle

spool of thread

pennant

Munching Manatees

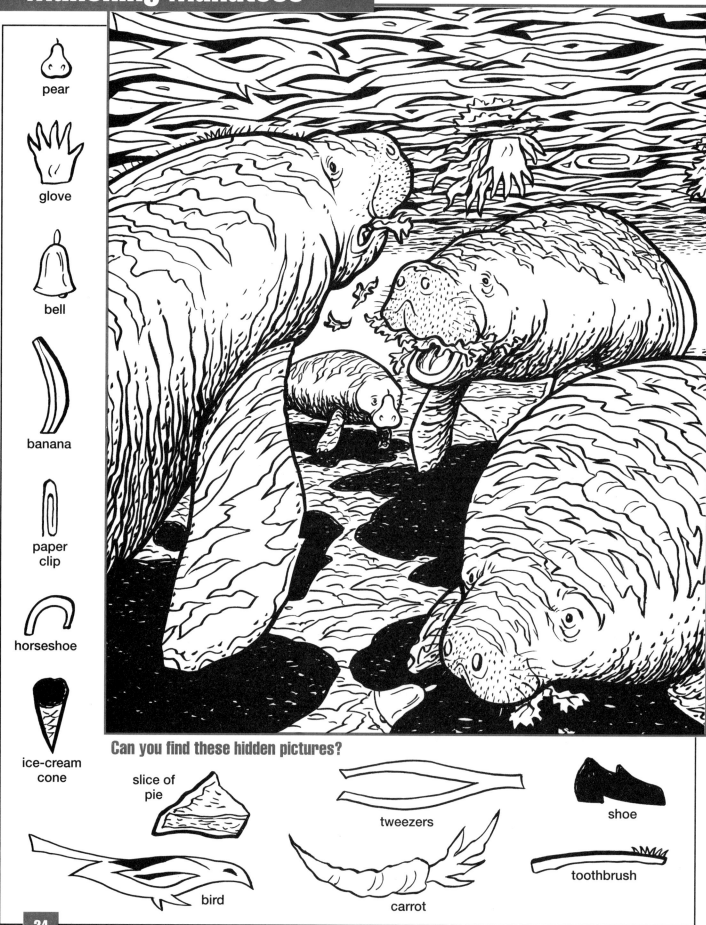

pear

glove

bell

banana

paper clip

horseshoe

ice-cream cone

Can you find these hidden pictures?

slice of pie

tweezers

shoe

bird

carrot

toothbrush

Illustrated by Timothy Davis

Highlights®

October 1, 2001, is Children's Day.

chef's hat

light bulb

nail

fish

hat

ice-cream pop

teacup

carrot

handbell

witch's hat

Can you find these hidden pictures?

candle

ice-cream cone

flag

baseball bat

Illustrated by Janet Robertson

Highlights®

slice of cake

ice-cream cone

open book

pennant

carrot

Can you find these hidden pictures?

teacup

magnifying glass

mitten

spoon

bell

feather

acorn

Highlights®

Pet Pride

sock

artist's brush

elf's hat

carrot

ring

toothbrush

tack

swan

snail

ruler

banana

ax

Can you find these hidden pictures?

PET SHOW

RUFF + TUMBLE

Bubbles

Princess

BLAZE

1

Highlights®

Little Shavers

sailboat

light bulb

heart

paper clip

saw

T-shirt

Can you find these hidden pictures?

hockey stick

banana

rabbit

snail

fishhook

fish

pencil

pine tree

shovel

dragonfly

Illustrated by Timothy Davis

Highlights®

April Fools' Day is on a Sunday this year.

Surprise Package

yo-yo

pushpin

hose

banana

hat

wooden shoe

cherry

trowel

rabbit's head

Can you find these hidden pictures?

apple

ladle

pennant

artist's brush

spoon

Highlights®

Golfing Buddies

key

fishhook

mushroom

acorn

radish

Can you find these hidden pictures?

spoon

nail

hammer

mitten

musical note

spatula

ice-cream cone

bat

eyeglasses

artist's brush

slice of pie

candle

toothbrush

pencil

hammer

ghost

crescent moon

nail

saltshaker

teacup

tack

crown

Can you find these hidden pictures?

Illustrated by R. Michael Palan

Highlights®

Tropical Trio

September is National Piano Month.

ruler

light bulb

hammer

handbell

toothbrush

sneaker

banana

crown

Illustrated by Timothy Davis

Can you find these hidden pictures?

truck

scissors

eyeglasses

teacup

saw

fish

glove

heart

pencil

32

Highlights®

Dinnertime Magic

slipper

sailboat

duck

sock

cap

hatchet

tea bag

frying pan

bird

ring

mushroom

fish

Can you find these hidden pictures?

hammer

spatula

closed umbrella

dinosaur's head

Highlights®

rabbit

shoe

witch's hat

paper clip

mitten

musical note

slice of pie

Can you find these hidden pictures?

goose

spoon

golf club

alligator

mouse

bird

artist's brush

tadpole

pencil

Illustrated by Timothy Davis

chicken

carrot

pliers

banana

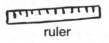

ruler

2 fish

penguin

flag

fish

rabbit's head

ruler

carrot

cracker

Can you find these hidden pictures?

spatula

needle

horn

ring

clock

baby's bottle

bowl

squirrel

candle

caterpillar

kite

butter knife

ruler

coffeepot

mitten

banana

Can you find these hidden pictures?

screwdriver

crescent moon

funnel

spatula

shoe

Marsh Melody

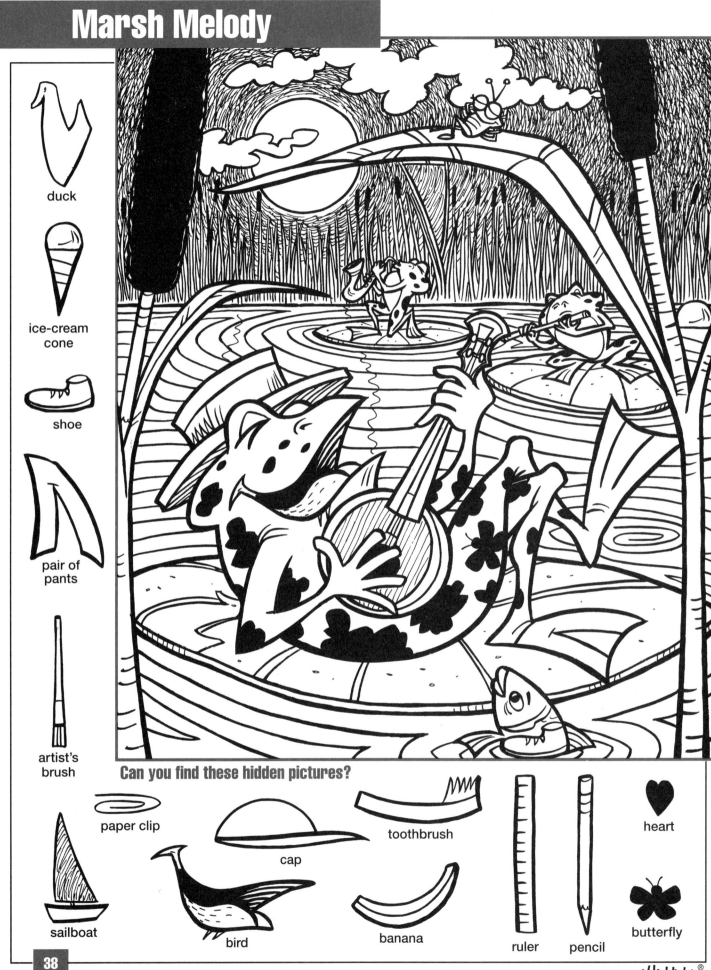

duck

ice-cream cone

shoe

pair of pants

artist's brush

Can you find these hidden pictures?

paper clip

sailboat

bird

cap

toothbrush

banana

ruler

pencil

heart

butterfly

Highlights®

Answers

▼Page 1

▼Page 2

▼Page 3

Highlights®

Answers

▼ Page 4

▼ Page 5

▼ Page 6

▼ Page 7

Highlights®

Answers

▼Page 8

▼Page 9

▼Page 10

▼Page 11

Highlights®

Answers

▼Page 12

▼Page 13

▼Pages 14-15

Highlights®

Answers

▼ Page 16

▼ Page 17

▼ Page 18

▼ Page 19

Highlights®

Answers

▼Pages 20-21

▼Page 22

▼Page 23

Highlights®

Answers

Highlights®

Answers

▼Page 28

▼Page 29

▼Page 30

▼Page 31

Highlights®

Answers

▼Page 32

▼Page 33

▼Pages 34-35

Highlights®

47

Answers

▼Page 36

▼Page 37

▼Page 38

▼Cover